# NIGHT BIRDS

&

# OTHER STORIES

## KHET MAR

*Translated by Maung Maung Myint*

A SAMPSONIA WAY™ PUBLICATION I SAMPSONIAWAY.ORG
IMPRINT OF CITY OF ASYLUM

Published by Sampsonia Way,
the publishing arm of City of Asylum
330 Sampsonia Way
Pittsburgh, Pennsylvania 15212-4440

www.sampsoniaway.org
www.cityofasylumpittsburgh.org

Sampsonia Way Managing Editor: Silvia Duarte
Book design: Michael Solano-Mullings
Cover artwork: Paw Thame
Cover design: Michael Solano-Mullings

# NIGHT BIRDS
## and Other Stories

# Night Birds

*Khet Mar wrote* Night Birds, *her second short novel, in 1993. The reader might be surprised to know that this piece was banned. At first glance, it is simply the story of two teenagers, oppressed by family members and confined to two tiny apartments. They can talk only through their windows. However, the Press Scrutiny and Registration Division of the Ministry of Information—the Burmese government's censorship department—understood that the story was a metaphor. As Khet Mar recognizes, the story was "a fictional way to express what happened to me in jail."*

# 1

It was listening to your songs that first gave me so much pleasure.

If you could recall the sky that morning, it would have completely mesmerized you. I remember that morning quite vividly—it was unforgettable.

The fog was so thick, Chu. No light broke through, the air impenetrable to the eye. A car drove through that thick mass of fog, stopping in front of the building next to yours.

I was sitting in the front seat of that car. I looked at the driver; he eyed me back, both of us knowing what we had to do next. We opened the car doors simultaneously and got out. He reached the staircase first, standing, as he was, closer to the building than I. I walked around the front of the car through the thick haze, following him to the staircase.

It was such a narrow staircase with shoddily-made cement steps. We walked up. First landing, second landing. First floor, second floor, third, fourth. I lost count. I tried to imagine the place we were headed. I had no idea where this staircase would lead me or what kind of place it was.

My legs were tiring and the yellow backpack on my back growing heavy when the man stopped in front of a door and unlocked a huge lock.

*Click*

The sound of the lock was subtle, yet struck a note of fear in me—it was scary not to know how many hours, days or even months I would have to spend behind this door.

My legs didn't want to move. My heart beat unevenly. Unfamiliar muscles in my body rebelled, pulling me back from the room.

"Come. Come inside." His voice was as cold as the air in the room.

I could barely nod, let alone utter an assent. I stepped onto the bare concrete floor and looked around the room.

It was a large, open room, about 50 x 13 feet, with no partitions. There was a separate so-called kitchen, and I spied a bedroll and a water pot on the right side of the room lying silently on the rough floor.

"There are some utensils in the kitchen. Your food will be sent here in a tiffin box every morning. If you need anything, just tell the man who brings your meals. I'll come back and check in every now and then. Do you hear me?"

In an atmosphere already chilled by the winter and the thick mist, his voice chilled me even more. I didn't respond. I didn't think I needed to, and besides, I didn't want to. I glared at him, trying to convey my anger, humiliation and how much I despised him all in that one look, but was so tired I'm not sure my eyes were able to deliver the message.

I slid my backpack off my shoulder and untied the bedroll, loosening the red plastic strings. As I unfolded the mat, a thick green-striped cotton blanket, a small pillow and a thin cotton blanket appeared.

My heart dropped when I saw these. I realized my mother had arranged these things for me as best as she could, trying to protect me not only from the hard winter weather, but also from the coldness of human beings. I felt tears surge into my eyes and batted my eyelashes, trying to chase them back. I turned my back to the bedroll and began to unzip my backpack when I heard him speak again.

"I'm leaving now. Don't try anything funny. I'll be back when I feel like it, and I want to see that you've been behaving."

I heard his voice but paid no attention to his face, neither raising my head to look at him, nor responding verbally. I kept busy with the zipper of my backpack. I knew my requests would be ignored, just by the fact of me being here, but I could still assert myself by refusing to do things I didn't want to do.

As I pulled my grey sweatshirt from my backpack, I heard him walking away. I heard his feet shuffling and the jangling of his keys. I heard the hinges creak as he shoved the door shut with his body. I froze, listening, all my senses tuned to every tiny sound.

*Click*

"Ohhh." My breath escaped me, the first sound to come out of my mouth since I entered the room, and I felt a sudden twinge in my chest—shock, hatred, despair and a desire for revenge all converging to leaving me breathless. How could he be so cruel?

He had locked the room with me inside! He left me alone in this room, the sole living being!

I hurled my backpack to the floor. Rage exploded like a bomb in my head. I rushed to the door and began pounding on it over and over again, unrelentingly, slamming it with my palms and trying to ram it open with my shoulders, all the while screaming like a madman.

"What do you think you're doing? Open the door! Open it! Don't do this! It's not fair! You pig! You bastard!"

My hands were aching and bloody. The door remained shut, but trembled from my assault on it.

Maybe he's still there. Is he still there? Is he going to open the door? Because he feels badly for me? My mind entertained these questions only a brief moment before I knew the answers.

He's gone. He walked down the staircase. He's grinning, satisfied because he heard you straining at the door. Don't you realize he's a person who feeds off the mental sufferings of others?

Every joint in my body felt shattered. I felt as if some unknown force had sucked all the strength from my body. I sighed again, seeing my life stretched out before me, doomed to a future of hopelessness and endless suffering.

I gathered what strength I still had and rolled out my bed, finding a spot on the floor that was somewhat less filthy than the rest. I heard the distant sound of a car engine and, agitated, ran across the room, hoping to get a glimpse of the street.

I threw open a door and found a veranda about three feet wide which I stepped out onto, looking down to see where the noise had come from.

The thick fog made it impossible to see anything other than the blue blur of the car that brought me here. The blur soon disappeared in the haze. Its disappearance strangely relieved me. As it slipped out of sight, the overwhelming coldness of my bitterness also retreated, along with the shock of this forced isolation.

Standing on the veranda, I decided to explore my surroundings. There was a small alley and a narrow driveway beneath me. Across the driveway, opposite my building, was a large plot of ground presumably to build a government building. Beneath me were the verandas of the rooms I had passed walking up the stairs. Above my head, the sky was a mixed haze of blue and white.

So, I was locked on the right side of the building on the very top floor. To the left of my room was the room on the opposite side of the stairway. Further left beyond that room was a space where an old house had been demolished. All that remained of it were some old pieces of scrap wood, a pile of sand and some bricks. Perhaps they were going to build the same type of building as the one I was currently locked inside.

To my right was a building designed like mine, composed of similar rooms except that those rooms did not have verandas wrapping around the front and side like my building did. An alley about six- or seven-feet-wide separated our two buildings. Except for this building, I was pretty much isolated. To the front, back and left of my building all was uninhabited.

So this was why he had brought me here. He figured this place would be the most suitable punishment for me. My thoughts ran back over the events that led me here.

With leaden steps, I walked back into the empty room and sank onto the thin red bed mat. At first I leaned my back against the brick wall but soon found myself lying flat out on the bed.

I lay there motionless for a while until my hands got cold. Then I put my hands between my head and the pillow to make them warm again. I recalled how my mom used to hold my hands softly and rub my palms to keep me warm and make me feel better. My heart ached as I lay there trying to conjure up a clear image of my mother.

How was she doing now?

———————

My mom shed her tears in silence and wiped them away with the back of her hand and the sleeves of her blouse. Except for occasional whimpering sounds, her crying was deprived of noise.

"Calm down, son. Calm down," she said, intending to comfort me, but her words reeked of despair. "Everything you've done so far has done no good. It's only escalated the situation between you and him. We can't escape him so easily. Your sister's only a teenager and still has to finish school."

"It's only you who don't know what to do. If you could only decide what you want," I replied. "We can break away! We can take control of our lives. We may become poor and go through some hard times, but we can deal with that. Make up your mind, Mom. Be brave."

I spoke those last words through clenched teeth, overwhelmed by the anger I held against her, almost forgetting I was talking to my own mother. I was aware I was committing an offense and might be punished in the next life for speaking so rudely to my mom, but to me, suffering in the next life was preferable to suffering in this one.

"I have so many reasons keeping me here, Son. How can I explain to you? For the time being our lives are in his hands.

Do you think, even if we managed to get out from under his shadow, that we could be free from his influence? He'd be out for revenge and would stop at nothing. He's ruthless. The hatred of a man like him could destroy all of our lives."

"Only now, after years of heartbreak, you recognize that he's ruthless? It's too late—he's already destroyed us."

"I'm not saying you're wrong, Son. But you're young. You want to rebel and be free. But," she continued, "the person you want to confront is a wicked man. Please don't forget that. I wish you wouldn't resist him so hard. No matter how bad he is, he's still in the role of your father."

"No!" I shouted. "Don't say that! There's no way I could ever accept him as my father! Maybe if you had married him out of love," my words were cruel, "but you married him just because of our situation, because of his power and high standing. He might be your husband, but he's no relation to my sister or me. A stepfather is a stepfather. No matter how desperately he wants to be or act like our father, he's still a stepfather."

My mother was crying. I glared at her: "This is nonsense! We are in this situation because you can't decide what to do. How can we stand idly by and do nothing against his behavior?"

My mom met my look, shaking her finger at me, "Yes, but do you know why I did what I did? Don't you understand? Whatever I did, I did it to help my children. I meant well, even if it went wrong. What can I do now? There's no getting away."

Her lips trembled. "You know how he threatens us, how cruel he can be. The whole family will suffer if we try to escape. You're a young man; maybe you're not afraid to face all those difficulties, but you have to understand—your mother is an old women who has lost her strength and spirit," she said. Her voice was sad, but also carried an anger born of love.

"Your sister is only a teenager. Do you want to see us suffer from this man's retribution? Don't think for a second that you're the only one who suffers. We all have hearts and souls familiar with suffering, but there are situations in life that require timing and consideration. Do you understand?"

My mother's words left me speechless. I felt awkward and sad and wondered what to say, how to get out of this dilemma. Situations require timing and consideration. So we're just supposed to keep living under his cruelty then? I knew we had to do something. I had tried to do something, but everything I tried failed.

At first when I was younger, he'd overpowered me completely with his violence, his fists, his abusive, needling words. As man of the house, he had all the authority, while I was just a kid, not yet fully educated, with people to care for. Our confrontations had always ended in failure for me. I sensed the same stench of failure now.

I was about to walk out on my mother when he appeared at the door. He strode deliberately toward me, an ugly sneer on his face, "So, you hate me so much? You want to hurt me? You can't bear living with me? All right. Pack your bags. I'll take you somewhere where you'll never have to see my face again. We'll leave in the morning."

He disappeared into his bedroom. My mother and I exchanged a fleeting, silent look. Her face swam in tears and confusion.

I was confused too. Should I take refuge where I'd never have to see his face again? Or should I turn down such an offer from a person I hated? If I turned it down, could I put up with his fists, his black looks, the brutalities that were sure to follow without fighting back? Me, who was so quick-tempered and fast to respond to any sign of injustice?

The problem was that I knew him very well. If I rejected his plan, he would punish my regret-ridden mother and my innocent younger sister. It would hurt my family. I sighed, unsure what to do. My mother was watching me, wondering.

"I'll let him take me to this place he's talking about. I want to go where I don't have to see him. I'll stay there and find a way out of this," I told her. My mom looked at me speechless, her mouth hanging open, reduced to a sort of shocked paralysis.

I walked past her and tried to imagine what tomorrow would bring. A cold, locked room was not what I had expected.

# 2

As my reflections, dominated by despair and anger, ended, an infernal sleep accompanied by a series of nightmares began.

By the time I woke up, a dark night had already kicked in. Exhausted, I began moving around, my feet taking me aimlessly about the room.

Where do I go? What do I think?' What do I do? How do I spend my time here?

My undirected footsteps led me to the veranda. I walked along it, and as I reached the front corner, I heard a song.

"Don't despair. The Lord Buddha will show his sympathy. Perhaps we will meet again in the next life."

The sharp, clear voice cut through my stupor, snapping me to full alert. All my attention was directed toward the extraordinary singing of this female voice.

My feet stood still as my eyes searched the direction from which the voice had come. Most everything around me was covered with darkness.

In the building beside me, I saw a few quiet apartments. Some had their doors open; others were closed. Some were well lit by florescent lights, while others gloomed beneath the reddish glow of tungsten bulbs.

Bending over the handrail, I searched methodically for the singer, screening the adjacent building bottom to top, every floor, every room.

The melancholy song continued, drifting elegantly through the air. I wondered why the singer, whom I believed to be young, sang this type of song with such fervor.

My eyes found and traced a path toward a window on the same floor as mine. I could see only a blurry image. It was a small, barred window with a single out-swinging shutter. Behind the bars, I saw the shadowy figure of a head. A reddish tungsten bulb hanging from the ceiling behind the head created the silhouette of a girl with flowing hair.

The moment I identified the silhouette as the singer-girl, the singing stopped. The silhouetted head remained motionless. Unconsciously, I walked a little faster along the veranda to the spot directly opposite the shadow. She started singing again.

*"When emerging sunrays shine, yeah, this is Sagaing Road."*

My interest mounted. My hands automatically searched for guitar chords in the air. I missed my guitar and the freedom associated with it—sitting on the street corners with my friends and playing. I missed everything. Running my fingers along the guitar strings was an important part of my life. Without it, I felt like a part of my body had been amputated.

Gazing at the singer-girl whose face I couldn't see, I sat down on the floor of the veranda and leaned my back against the wall. The night was growing darker, and the cold winter air made my muscles cramp up.

The block guard struck the metal bars once, a striking metallic sound indicating that it was one hour past midnight. No longer able to withstand the cold, I stood up. She must have seen me, as the singing stopped again.

Because I hadn't turned on the light in my room, I was standing in darkness with only the dim light of a distant lamppost shining on me.

My boldness grew. I moved my lips. The cold wind had made them dry and numb.

"Hello." No response or movement. I picked up my spirits and continued, "I cannot see your face, but you sang really well." The silhouetted figure remained motionless and quiet.

"I've been listening to you all evening, but I'm going to bed now. Thanks for your songs." Not expecting a response from the shadow, I walked back around the veranda and toward my room.

It was pitch-black inside. I searched for the light switch, which I soon found on the wall next to my bed. An amber bulb lit up over the veranda where I had just been sitting. I bent my head to look for the light in the singer-girl's window. There was another door at the foot of my bed that opened out onto the veranda opposite her window.

I found another light switch. With a click, a bulb over my head lit up. I didn't like the tungsten light, but it was all I had. Looking down at a room well lit with fluorescent light, I noticed that the light had disappeared from the singer-girl's window.

Maybe she went to bed, embracing her songs. I lay down on the mat feeling a cold hardness underneath my back and knew I wouldn't get much sleep that night.

---

The first thing I did when I woke up from that dreadful night's sleep was to walk over to the door to look out at the window from which last night's songs had overflowed.

"Oh." The soulless window welcomed me with a cold grace. I stepped quickly back inside away from the bitter cold.

The sound of someone unlocking the huge metal lock that kept me trapped inside startled me. I paced back and forth, feeling ashamed for being frightened. Had my spirit been so diminished that the sound of a door being unlocked could frighten me?

The door opened. I saw two hands and then a man's head with dark skin and expressionless eyes, as he came inside.

"Here." He extended his hand toward me with a steel tiffin box. Seeing me unmoved by his offer, he placed the box on the floor. "Do you want me to bring anything?"

I answered immediately, "Guitar. Bring me my guitar."

The dark-skinned man nodded and quickly left. I heard the door close and the key turn in the lock. I listened to his steps tread heavily down the staircase. All of a sudden I was lonely again.

By the time I finished eating my cold breakfast, the sun's rays had scorched away the thick veil of fog. My eyes returned to the window, and my heart started pounding really fast. It was because I saw you there, Chu.

I saw you through the side window of your white room. The distance between the buildings wasn't more than six or seven feet, so I could see your upper body clearly.

You were wearing a large white shirt. Your hair was down. Perhaps you had just washed it. The white-washed wall, the white shirt and the black long hair falling on your shoulders all made you look like one of those angelic beings I had read about in children's stories.

You noticed me too and gave me a brief curious look. Then you smiled. It was so pure—the way your purple lips curled up, the way your white teeth sparkled like pearls, the way a mole over your upper lip moved. I watched every detail as if you were in a movie. You were mysteriously attractive.

"Are you a new one?" Your voice didn't fit your physical appearance. It wasn't the least bit soft or willowy as I expected, but more hard and tough. I began to doubt if you were indeed last night's singer-girl. Unsure, I nodded my head.

"Good, good," you said. I never asked you why you said that. I never asked myself either. I was in such a hurry to talk with you.

"Was it you, little lady, who sang the songs?"

You laughed. "So, you call me little lady. How old do you think I am?" You had answered my question with a question, but it didn't bother me at all. In fact it intrigued me more.

"I can't guess your age. But I can tell you mine. Today is December 21. On January 13, I'll be 23."

"So, it's not too long until your birthday then. Maybe I'll have some kind of celebration for you. I'm seven years older than you. My birthday is August 29," you replied.

I wondered if it were true that you were older than me, but your face shone with candor. Instantly, we felt very close.

"Even though I'm seven years younger than you, I'll still call you little lady just because maybe I'm a little presumptuous."

I was very pleased to have such a companion, so interesting and mysterious. My feelings seemed to be reciprocated. Your eyes brightened as we talked.

"Did you hear what I said last night?" I asked you.

"Of course. Our rooms are close, and the night was silent. I heard you well. I guess you also heard my singing well?"

"Yes. That's why I tried to talk to you, even though I couldn't see. I didn't know I had a light on my wall, you see. I was kind of afraid that my voice coming from the dark might frighten you, but I had to say something because you sang really well."

"Thank you so much for your compliments. Yes, I was frightened by your sudden voice. I thought no one was in that room. That's why I stopped singing and went to bed."

As the background noise was louder in the daytime, we had to raise our voices to be heard. My heart was content talking with you, Chu. You were the only living being near me at that moment, even though walls separated us.

"Do you sing every night?"

"I do, almost every night."

"Then there are nights when you don't sing? What do you do those nights? Go to bed early?" You didn't reply. After a while you said evenly, "I love nights. I never go to bed early. Some nights I don't sleep at all. You will be staying in this room for a while, won't you? You'll know what I do on the nights I don't sing."

I didn't ask any more questions. I understood that I had no other choice except to watch your nights.

---

During the many nights that followed, I became familiar with your songs.

That clear, low-pitched, vibrant voice of yours made my heart beat faster. While you were singing, I imagined my left fingers skimming over the fretboard of my guitar, searching for the chords. I felt nostalgic whenever I heard you sing.

I craved my guitar and the freedom I had lost. You continued to sing as if you didn't notice my moods.

The first song you would sing was "Restful Sleep." Sometimes you'd choose "Far Away Salween" instead. Your voice seemed to vibrate in time with the echoes of your heartbeats. Well, at least it vibrated in time with my heartbeats, Chu.

*"Your command, I don't want to defy."*

I soon understood that Kyaw Hein's "Command" was one of your favorites. You sang that song every night.

It was a great fun for me to imagine the day I'd surprise you by accompanying your singing with my guitar. I could barely contain myself thinking about it and how happy it would make you, and I had to remind myself constantly to keep my plan secret so as not ruin your surprise.

But my guitar hadn't arrived yet. I had forgotten that the man who told me to say if I needed anything was a man who enjoyed mentally torturing people before fulfilling their needs.

"Hey, are you sleeping?" Whenever you didn't feel like singing, you'd try to strike up a conversation. That gave me permission to speak too. I didn't want to interrupt your singing.

"No, I'm not. I'm waiting to speak with you," I said.

"All right. About what?" you asked.

"Chu . . . why don't you sing on stage? You have such great talent." For the first time, I heard you laugh. Although it was the sound of laughter it was neither exactly happy nor particularly feminine. It was loud, harsh and a bit jarring, not at all rhythmical, reminding me of the stilted "Ha Ha" one reads in books.

"I couldn't go on stage. Just singing what I want to sing makes my life complete. Sure, I want other people to hear and feel my songs. And until recently, I only entertained myself. It's nice you are here now. You are my only audience."

"Why can't you perform for a bigger audience?"

You avoided my question. "We'll have plenty of time to talk, won't we? I'll tell you later. Let's change the topic."

Someone somewhere struck the metal bars to mark the arrival of midnight. One. Two. Three. As I counted the metallic clangs, I tried to find another topic. Another topic. Another topic. "Have you sung on stage before?" Well, that wasn't exactly another topic.

"I did. A few years ago, Khaing Chu May was a stage-singer with a considerable fan base who entertained at university dinners and township stage shows."

"What kind of songs do you like to sing best?" (I was relieved that you had answered my question but still tried to divert the conversation slightly.)

"I want to sing the songs of Khaing Htoo."

"Right, there are not many girls who can sing Khaing Htoo's songs. You are a special one."

"I like his voice very much, also his lyrics."

At this point we fell silent. Naturally, I was more curious about the topic you didn't want to talk about.

I started thinking about what your life must be like—your isolated life. With the exception of a young girl I had seen briefly in your apartment during the week, you were more or less alone.

Your full name was Khaing Chu May. This much you had told me without even being asked. I started thinking about your choice of songs. I was certain your exquisite voice would thrill your audiences.

It was hard to contain my curiosity. I had to keep reminding myself not to ask you questions you didn't want to answer yet, so I decided to put an end to the night's chat.

"Well, the night's getting late. Let's take a rest."

"Okay, goodnight."

"Goodnight, goodnight."

I wished you a wonderful night, Chu. I wanted you to have sweet dreams that night. As I knew my thoughts wouldn't disturb your sleep I allowed myself to think about you.

*3*

"**W**hat do you see in the sky in front of you? Please tell me."

You asked me that one of those nights you didn't sing. I was kind of reluctant to answer. I could see the sky behind your building, and, standing facing me, you could see the sky behind mine.

"I see a bunch of white clouds over the right corner of your apartment. It looks like a big white balloon flower; it's very beautiful," I said. "I also see TV antennas here and there."

As I finished talking, a trail of smoke drifted through your window bars.

You were smoking. I could envision your purple lips.

"Can't you see the moon?"

I tried searching for the moon on your request. "I don't see the moon. Do you?"

"No. I don't."

You craned your neck, trying to find the moon. Perhaps it was shining somewhere in the sky where neither you nor I could see. We saw the light given off by the moon though.

"Tell me, Chu, what do you see on your side of the sky?" I got a good dose of your non-poetic laughter as a reply.

"Darker sky, groups of clouds scattering here and there, some stars. Oh, there is one other thing. I can see a big tree branching out towards the sky. I've seen it so many times but still can't figure out what kind of tree it is. I love thinking about it, trying to figure it out," you said.

"Hey, Chu. I can see a dark blurry shape from my side of the sky. It could be a water tower." I got no response. I had no clue what you were thinking, and it made me realize that even if I couldn't make you happy, I wanted you to be at ease, with no worries in your mind, Chu.

"No birds?" Your voice, accompanied by cigarette smoke, came through the bars again, slightly trembling and frail. I became more anxious for you.

"You don't see birds at night. Do you wish to see birds?"

"Yes, sometimes it does my mind good to watch the birds fly. I would envy them, yet I feel happy for them because they are flying. Sometimes I can become furious because of it," you said.

I didn't know what to say to take away your sadness. I was worried that if we continued talking about birds, it might bring up the word "freedom" and remind you of your situation and the loneliness of your room.

"Not even a night-bird?" Your voice flowed into the night air. Except for the chirping sound of crickets, there was total silence.

I was addicted to your non-poetic voice. Your voice made my life complete, and the nights without your voice felt meaningless to me.

But tonight, because I cared about you, I had to try to stop you from talking about birds, to change the tone of sadness in your voice. So I said, "Chu, aren't you going to sing tonight?"

"No, dear. I don't want to."

"Why not?"

"Once in a while, it feels meaningless for me to sing. Why do I sing? For whom do I sing? I never get an answer to those questions, and I don't want to sing when I feel that way."

I realized I wouldn't be able to coax any feelings of freedom and life out of you tonight. All my words just further burdened your mind—a mind already overloaded with sadness. So I ended the night's talk.

"Well, it's getting cold. You should close your doors."

"I will soon. I'm just trying to find a few night birds."

I sighed quietly, exhausted by it all. Your face, faintly illuminated by the light reflecting off the walls of my building, was shadowed by the window bars. Your eyes were shrouded by cigarette smoke. I wanted to see your eyes clearly as you said those words.

Why were you so lonely, Chu? Why should such a beautiful young girl like you, so vibrant, spend your life in a tiny apartment?

I tried to imagine your future. A piece of the sky, a chunk of land, a small window, some cigarettes, a few songs and me, your temporary friend. Were these all the possessions in your life? You should have more than that, Chu.

"Although we find ourselves so close to each other, the sky we see is so different." You rekindled our conversation, ending your poetic sentence with a non-poetic laugh.

I pondered your words. They made me sad.

You were right, Chu. We saw different things. We should at least have been able to see the same sky, shouldn't we?

———————

I heard the sound of footsteps around lunchtime but had no idea they would be so foreboding.

I had stopped paying much attention to the now-familiar sound of the door opening. However, this time it was flung open, and the person on the other side stormed into the room.

It was him. The man whose face I despised. It was stony as he entered the room. I was actually grateful to him for leaving me alone in this tiny room for more than ten days.

And what was this! Behind him I saw someone else entering: The hand that brought me my lunchbox every day was now carrying my guitar, the golden-brown guitar I had held in my hands so many times. Forgetting everything at that moment, even my own existence, I rushed to take my guitar. My fingers darted up and down the slack strings.

"Do you want to go back home?" My stepfather's voice echoed in the room, stunning my hands into silence. I replayed the words. He had asked me if I wanted to go home!

But the home I wanted to return to was a home with only my mother, my sister and me—no one else. I didn't want to go back to a home controlled ruthlessly by someone who had paralyzed my family to the point they didn't even dare speak or move.

"Hey! Didn't you hear me?"

As I had no answer to give, I didn't answer him. I focused all my attention on the guitar. Rhythm, chords, bars, keys—I would rather live with them.

*Whack!*

His slap left my right cheek burning. My body moved reflexively, but I managed to control my temper.

It was nothing new. I was accustomed to it—his insults, his cruelty, the violence. I had tried to escape them many times, but my love for my family always prevented me from leaving. How would my mother feel if I left? How would he treat my sister who was still young? I was caught in a vicious circle.

"We'll see who wins in the end—your stubbornness against my toughness."

He laughed viciously. How could my mom and my sister live with him? I thought about them struggling under his iron hand.

"I want to see my mother and sister." His eyes flared up at my request. His lips twisted into some perversion of a smile. He jeered, "You'll see them when the time comes."

Without saying anything more, he left with the lunch-man, slamming the door with a deafening crash. A key turned and locked it. I listened to his footsteps storming hard down the stairs.

Now it was my turn to smile. What an egomaniac! He couldn't even take me ignoring him, let alone tolerate serious dissent. Look how hard he hit me. I wondered sadly whether this world was becoming overpopulated with such cold-blooded, sadistic thugs.

Even so, I was grateful to him for bringing my guitar. During this time of self-chosen incarceration, it would be my best companion. I also hoped it would foster the bond of friendship and affection that was growing between Chu and myself. I wanted to share with her whatever bright spot I could find in the middle of this dark situation.

That was the longest evening, Chu, waiting for you. It seemed like the sun would never set and the night would never fall. The neighborhood was bustling with people and noise, and you were nowhere to be seen. I thought about sending you some kind of signal to bring you to the window.

Staring at your window was useless and gave me no encouragement at all. The amber tungsten bulb remained unlit. Even when I turned on my veranda light, your room remained silent. I kept peering through your window, but you were nowhere to be found.

The night was getting older. My excitement grew greater. How could you be so silent on this most amazing night, Chu? I thought of shouting out to let you know I was here.

I decided not to. After all, I didn't know what held you back. There was nothing I could do but wait.

*Yes!*

A flash of light, as you lit up a cigarette, and there was your face illuminated briefly in the yellow flame. Within a second, the window was partly shrouded in smoke. You were smoking again.

The way you smoked worried me. You'd light up one cigarette after another and keep up the chain for a long time, sometimes smoking through our whole conversation. It scared me, imagining the amount of cigarette smoke that passed through your lungs during our late-evening to early-morning talks. Even now, only a few minutes after nine o'clock, you had already begun smoking.

"Chu..."

"Yes."

The quickness of your response surprised me. "What are you doing there?"

"I've been here by the window for a while. I saw you."

"But I can't see you. Your room's dark. I can only see the cigarette smoke. Why are you just sitting there? Why do you smoke so much? Why don't you turn on the light?"

"I can't do much except think sitting here in the dark. And the reason for not turning on the light is because I like to sit in the dark."

Sitting in the dark thinking? Uh-oh. That was a clear sign I'd need to do something to keep you from spending a long night with depressing thoughts.

"Why don't you sing, Chu?"

"What do you want me to sing?"

"Whatever you like. Most of your songs are nice."

You laughed lightly. It made me happy.

"Can you turn off your light?"

"Why?"

"I don't want to see the light. Wouldn't it be nice to feel the song differently by hearing it come out of the darkness?" you asked.

I was always ready to do anything to make you happy, Chu. So I went inside and turned off the light. You had already started singing when I came back to the veranda.

*"Yearning to go back home,"*
*"I left my home on a foggy night when snow started falling"*

My legs froze. My knees trembled. Why that song, Chu? Did you mean to sing it for me? Except . . . I hadn't told you I'd left home on a foggy day. Maybe you were singing this song for yourself? Did you also leave your home? Were you also yearning to go back?

Tonight, I thought, it was time for us to tell each other about our lives.

I snapped out of my thoughts, though, remembering my guitar. I snatched it up and started playing just in time for the second verse.

*"A challenging road ahead,*
*Scorching through the thorny field"*

The sudden strum of the strings caught you off guard. You stopped singing.

"Chu, don't stop. Keep singing. Keep singing." I continued playing my guitar.

*"Though there is a way to cease the tragedies,*
*It's nowhere near"*

Even as you continued, you looked thrown off—your voice hesitant and your style a bit shaky. I played along patiently, waiting for you to recover. It's no wonder you were surprised. I understand it. Gradually your voice became robust again with its usual charisma.

My heart beat faster. I closed my eyes while I played, imagining you on stage. Young and self-confident, you were performing at the peak of your abilities—not only singing, but also communicating your love of freedom and the joy of music. The audience applauded and cheered. The cameras flashed and colorful spotlights lit your body. Your powerful voice commanded the air surrounding the stage.

*"Knowing that my old mother would be waiting to see me on the road home,*
*I still can't come back home"*

That verse made my heart flinch, recalling my mom's teary eyes as if she were standing right in front me.

I had to focus hard not to miss the chords. Everything was getting all mixed up in my mind. Chu, Khaing Chu May, the stage, the audience, applause, camera flashes, spotlights, Chu's smile, my happiness, my mom's tears, my sister's innocent smile, my music and Chu's clear voice.

*"In my thoughts and in my dreams*
*I went home.*
*I am yearning to go back home"*

Your clear voice faded away in the dark. My guitar music rose and fell a bit more with the night breeze before it finally came to halt.

As if we had made a deal in advance, we stayed silent for a while after the song and music subsided. I noticed tear drops on the guitar. I didn't think you could see me crying because the veranda light was turned off, so I wiped them off in the dark.

"Are you crying?" you asked.

Your question took me aback. Could you know I was crying? I didn't think so. You couldn't see my tears in this darkness. "No, I'm not." I replied. It was a lame response.

"Are you crying, Chu?" I asked.

"No, I'm not," you replied, your voice frail.

I worried—What had I done? I meant for the guitar to brighten up our nights and make them more cheerful, to bring music into your lonely life. Yet instead it had brought tears and sadness. But I had brought the guitar with good intentions, and on that solemn word implored that your sadness would disappear.

"Where did you get that guitar?" Your voice was firm again, so I was happy to answer.

"Someone from home sent it to me."

"Home?"

"Yes."

You asked no more. I thought I heard you sigh. How could I stop you from feeling sad on my behalf?

"I'm sorry. I didn't notice this wasn't your home. Please forgive me if my song stirred up your feelings in any way."

"No, Chu. It's all good, our times together. We sang to relieve ourselves from boredom. I'm happy. Please don't feel sad," I said, adopting a breezy tone.

I pretended that nothing bad had ever happened to me. I lied, but it was a white lie. A well-intentioned untruth to make you feel better.

"You say that you are happy, but my song was not a joyful song."

"Well, let's sing some joyful songs then." You went silent again. I tried to come up with some songs for you to sing.

"I can no longer sing joyful songs, you know," you said after a while.

I wanted to curse myself. Nothing I said made you happy. Why did I always choose words that caused you pain? I tried to make things right.

"Don't think too much, Chu. We shouldn't spend our time just thinking. Let's sing one more song. I still want to play guitar."

I waited anxiously for your response. Finally, you started singing another song.

It was . . . "The Last Dream."

# 4

Our nights were mostly warm and pleasant. I tried my best to keep it that way. We filled the hours with talking, singing, sharing our thoughts.

That night was one of those nights we didn't sing. My guitar leaned against the wall. You sat beneath your tungsten bulb. I could see you clearly that night, as both the light from your room and the glow from the bulb above my head shone on you.

You wore a loose, wrinkled, white sport shirt; your hair was pulled back and tied at the nape of your neck, making your flawless face more visible. I could see your glittering eyes and all the features of your face distinctly: narrow bluish eyes, a small, prominent mole—all the things that together made you so vibrant. You were listening to me, hanging on my every word; I could see your rapt attention even in the veins elevated and running along the back of your fists as they gripped the window bars.

"My mom's a very simple, honest woman, but she's had bad luck. My dad was addicted to drinking. He liked alcohol more than he liked her. It was his love for alcohol that killed him. My mom was left behind."

I thought about the X-ray that showed my father's severely damaged liver and could remember how worried my mother looked, and the naive eyes of my sister. I knew then that my sister and I would soon be fatherless. However, we had no idea that someone so cruel and cunning would take over the role of my father so soon.

"My mother's submissive nature probably made her an easy prey for his wickedness. A drunken father replaced by an evil stepfather. We tried our best to keep the peace at home. I tried to befriend him, and my sister showed him respect.

"But it was hard to change his innate personality. His harshness and brutality deepened my family's suffering. My mother was repeatedly humiliated, shouted at and beaten in front of us. Our attempts to defend her were also beaten down by brute force.

"'Your mom is officially my wife now!' he'd say. 'I can do as I please. Is that understood?' He was merciless, and my mom, whenever he said those things, would just look at him with those pathetic pleading eyes. I ended up with black eyes if I tried to confront him.

"All I really knew how to do was play a guitar. I was just a teenager trying to earn a college degree so I could get a job and earn money to support my family.

"But him—he was a grown man capable of using overwhelming force to intimidate us. It's no surprise we were constantly in tears. And then he'd amuse himself by staring at us with his deceitful smile. We'd console each other by wiping the tears from our faces.

"In the beginning, he tormented us with rude gestures. Then it was insults and abusive words. Physical abuse soon followed. We got used to his punches, slaps and beatings.

"I would threaten to leave the house, but my sister would plead not to leave them behind.

"My family bonds were too strong; I couldn't leave them. My sister and I talked my mother into filing for a divorce, but she just came back to us saying that she tried, but couldn't do anything because he wouldn't sign the divorce papers. Her words let us down.

"I suggested that we should all get away from the house together, my mother, sister and I.

"But my mother just said, 'Do you really believe that he won't find us?' Her words struck me hard. I knew better than anyone that he'd use his enormous influence to find us, and how he would punish us when he did.

"My mom worried that even if we did manage to escape, we wouldn't have anywhere to go, no way to make a living. She didn't see how we could start our lives from scratch, with her getting old and both of us still in school. I had a hard time listening to her worries. I knew we were in a dire situation.

"My father's drinking had put us in debt; it was made even worse by the medical expenses from his liver disease. My mother thought marrying this man would save our family. It wasn't long before we saw his true colors.

"My mom told me that if I wanted to get away, I'd have to do it alone. You could tell it made her sad, she spoke so slowly. My sister looked worried.

"How could I possibly leave my mother and sister behind?

"So we just all sighed. That was all we could do. My mom cried and said that we couldn't control our destiny. That we were condemned to continue our present suffering because of what we had done in our past. The hopelessness of her words essentially ended our conversation.

"I lay in bed that night trying to make a plan for my future. I had worked hard and tried my best to accept him as a family member and improve the atmosphere for the family, but I had failed miserably, and because of the things I did, he brought me here as punishment."

You listened to me patiently, not uttering a word until I was done telling my story. Had you been sitting beside me, I'm sure you would have whispered consolations in my ear. But since you were further away, I had to be content with the way you looked at me so compassionately.

"So, you can't attend your school now?" you asked sympathetically? You sounded worried.

"No, I can't."

"He shouldn't be so mean. He should at least care about your education."

"He might not want to see me become successful and independent with a degree and a job," I said. Chu, he already destroyed the hopes and dreams of three people. Why should he give a damn about my education?

"He's a cruel, deceitful, heartless man." I heard you sigh again.

The hopelessness of my future seemed to dishearten you as much as it did me. I hadn't intended to make you sad. I only wanted you to be happy, but I didn't have much happiness to share, so you got a good dose of my problems instead.

"You must fight back however you can against his oppression." Your voice was strong, tough, encouraging me. I looked up at you. You were sharing my pain, trying to cheer me up. Thank you, Chu.

"Yes, yes, I must," I said somewhat brusquely, acknowledging your support.

At that point we just burst out laughing. What else could we do about our miserable lives anyway, but laugh the pain away?

Sometimes I wanted to snap at you about your smoking, ask you why you smoke so much. I noticed, even from a distance, how purple your lips had become. But I didn't have the heart because I already knew the answer, and I didn't want to hear you say that you smoked because you were lonely.

I'd usually see the cigarette smoke in your room. Then I'd hear your voice. I could usually only see half your face beneath the weak tungsten light and a part of you through your room's small window. I couldn't see much of your surroundings or what your room looked like.

"There's a table beside my bed. On the table, there are two books of Buddha's teachings and a flower vase. There are some kitchen utensils on the other side of the bed and a water pitcher in the corner of the room. That's it," you told me.

Your abrupt end to your sentence made me try to think of a way to cheer you up.

"Got any flowers in that vase?"

"Yes, I do."

"Will you show them to me?"

You must have had the vase nearby. You bent to the side to pick it up and showed it to me through the window. The words I had ready on my lips to praise the flowers died on the spot. There was only a single red rose in the vase without even a leaf on the stalk!

"I prefer a single flower," you said, noticing my silence.

I sighed. What else could I do, Chu? I expected a bunch of flowers. I had wanted that for you. I remembered a large purple orchid tree I had seen near the back wall of my apartment. It may have been the biggest orchid tree I had ever seen. Its deep purple flowers were flourishing all over its branches, which nearly touched the wall.

"I have a big orchid tree in my backyard with deep purple flowers. Do you want some orchid flowers?"

"Those flowers don't really have much fragrance, do they?"

"I don't think much; sometimes a nice soft scent."

"Even if I say I want the flowers, how will you be able to give them to me?"

I calculated the distance between us. If I leaned my body over the railing and stretched out my arms, I could probably reach half the distance. The problem was on your side: Your window bars prevented you from leaning over, so there would be a gap between us even if you were able to stretch your arm out.

"I'll try to get a branch with a long stalk, so when I stretch it toward your window, it'll be long enough that you can just reach out and grab it."

"What if I ruin the flowers?"

"You might, but don't worry. I'll hand you the stalk side."

"I don't want it if it's a risk for you. It's 40 feet down. Just the thought of you falling scares me."

"It'll be all right," I said, ending the conversation and going to the back of my room. The flowers I wanted to give you weren't extravagant, but I'd be beyond happy if they meant something to you. I thought that flowers from a dungeon might have some symbolic value or bring with them some kind of inspiration.

It turned out to be somewhat difficult to get the flowers, though. The tree's highest branches were a bit below my reach. I tried to get a branch with a lot of flowers, so you'd have more than just one in your vase.

I finally managed to reach a branch with three fully-blooming purple orchids on it and some fresh buds, but the stalk wasn't long enough to reach you. It was frustrating to see the lovely flowers, so close yet so far away.

"Look at these flowers, aren't they beautiful?"

You responded with equal enthusiasm: "Oh, they are really beautiful, but the stalk is so short. How am I going to reach them?"

"Wait and see." I searched for a long thin piece of wood or something similar, but my room was scarce on things. All I found was a long-handled broom, so I inserted the stalk into the top of the broom handle. So far so good, but this way you'd have to grab the leaves or flower petals.

KHET MAR

I held on to the broom bristles, inclined my body over the veranda rail and extended my arm with the broom toward you. I reminded myself not to look down—I didn't want to be intimidated by the height.

"Don't bend over too far. You might fall. And make sure that that railing is strong enough to hold your weight," you cautioned me.

"I know. Just try to grab the branch. Go for the leaves or the flowers; better yet, try to reach the stalk."

You stretched your right arm through one of the small rectangular holes in the window bars and strained to reach the flower stalk. I was standing on tiptoe. My feet began to shake.

"Chu, grab the stalk."

"I can't. I can only touch one of the flowers."

Your arm was fully extended and your face pressed against the window bars, so you had to rely on your hands to feel whether you were touching flowers or leaves. I couldn't extend my hand any further either.

"Just grab the flower if you can reach it. Be careful though, please, so you don't crush it."

"Okay, just keep your hand steady. I have the flower now."

"Good. Hold it firm."

"Oh, no!'" I heard the distress in your voice and saw you look down.

Your eyes were following the branch, which was rapidly plummeting towards the ground. In your fist were a couple of crushed purple flower petals.

"It's gone. I lost it." Your whisper faded away. We looked into each other's eyes, our only way to console each other. We were too emotionally exhausted to say a word.

Holding the broom in my hand, I watched as the broken flower branch hit the ground, which welcomed it with a cold hard kiss.

# 5

**W**hen you told me your story, Chu, I found it completely enthralling.

It was pretty late when we started talking. You had sung a bunch of songs and were taking a break, cigarette between your lips. I was blowing on my sore fingertips to soothe them after some pretty intense playing.

There was no moonlight, but the stars kept the night sky pretty. Your room was dark, and so was mine. I had turned off my lights upon your request. Your face was only occasionally illuminated by the scant light from the hanging lamps on the street below. Your voice was remarkably clear that night.

"My story is similar to yours. I don't think that I can tell it as well as you did, but I'll tell you what I remember. My story also has a stepfather," you laughed. "We're both victims of stepfathers.

"But my father, unlike yours, didn't die. He just disappeared from our lives. He left my mom and me when I was about ten years old. I think I was in the sixth grade then.

"A few years later, we received a letter from him. He asked for forgiveness and said that he was praying for us. He said the trees where he now lived weren't evergreen, that they changed color in the different seasons. He said he longed for home when the seasons change, but he didn't write anything about coming back. I read the letter over and over again looking for the words "I am coming home," but I didn't find them. We don't know if he's still alive.

"My mother missed my father a lot, but she tried to hide it. She blamed him for choosing his own life over the family. To make a long story short, she waited for him several years, then remarried. My future stepfather's parents had approached my grandparents to convince them to let their son marry my mother. My grandparents believed that my mother's ambiguous marital status—neither a divorcée nor a widow—made her life miserable. So they talked her into marrying again.

"I don't know why my mom accepted that proposal. I always believed my father would come back to us someday. Maybe he just hasn't had a chance. It's hard to blame my mom for wanting to get married again.

"Up to then, I always thought about my father's return, when he would come back, and how we'd rebuild our relationship. All our misfortune came because of his disappearance and his not coming back.

"I'm not sure my mother's new husband counted as a stepfather because I'm not sure if my real father was still alive or not. My stepfather had a young man with him—I don't know if he was a nephew or an adopted son. I don't know because I never talked to my stepfather after he married my mom, and I avoided talking to my mother about her new husband. I tried my best to stay out of their way. Unfortunately, my mother became chronically sick soon after the wedding."

You told your story, Chu, in your own scattered way. I found it kind of charming. with surges of giddiness even, as your words tumbled over one another.

"Well, how shall I continue? Okay, let me tell it an easier way. One day my stepfather took my mother to a clinic. I was home alone playing guitar. I remember I was singing Khaing Htoo's song "The End of an Imaginary Kind Winter" and "Along with the Rhythm.""

"The young man came into the room while I was singing. I asked him what he was doing there, but he just laughed in a kind of nasty way, and I didn't like the leering look in his face. I asked him if my stepfather had sent him. 'Yes, of course,' he said, real cool-like. I was furious. I knew this kind of thing would happen to me some day. Well, I was ready for it."

You paused and lit a cigarette. It was excruciating to wait. I wanted to know how you ended up here, talking to me in the middle of the night.

"He said, 'They won't come back for a while. We planned it well.' I looked at him real calm, but my blood was running cold. He began to unbutton his shirt and said, 'It's too hot in here, don't you think?' I knew I had to do something then. I looked around the room to find some kind of weapon but couldn't find anything. I may have seemed calm on the outside, but I was boiling on the inside.

"He threw his shirt on the sofa, and when he turned toward me, I hit his head as hard as I could with my guitar. It made a huge banging sound. Then there was the sound of him falling on the table and the table legs breaking. He hit his head on the corner of the table, and it was bleeding. I thought to myself, I need to get out of here now.

"I wasn't so lucky though. He was lying face down on the floor near the front door, and as I was jumping over his body, trying not to step on his blood on my way out, my hesitation gave him a chance to act. He reached out and grabbed my ankles.

"I landed with a hard smack on the cement stairs in front of our apartment. I vaguely remember rolling down the stairs; it hurt so much I passed out. Later I was told that I kept rolling all the way down until I hit the pavement at the bottom. I had to spend a few months in the hospital. And now I will have to spend the rest of my life in a wheelchair."

I was completely stunned. I stared at you. Oh, my God! How could I not have known you were in a wheelchair? I was so stupid, so clueless. When we met, I asked you why you didn't sing on stage, and you said it was because you couldn't.

Maybe it was better that I hadn't realized it. My heart had already been deluged with concern for you, even before knowing the full extent of your misery. Now I had to find more room in my heart for your suffering.

I tried to forgive myself for my ignorance. The small window into your bedroom didn't allow me to see you that well. That's why I wasn't able to grasp your real situation.

You stayed silent, giving me time to overcome my surprise.

"Hey, are you still awake?" I heard your voice from the distance.

"Yes, yes." I responded, but didn't say anything else. I actually wanted to discontinue our conversation, so that I had more time to think about you.

"Did my story make you bored or disappointed?"

"No, not bored at all. I'm just thinking."

"What are you thinking?"

"I'm thinking about asking you a few questions, but I feel a bit awkward about it."

I heard you laugh softly. I looked around at the neighboring apartments. Only a few rooms were lit; most were dark. The entire neighborhood was pleasantly silent, indicating that most people were sound asleep. The quietness helped forge a closer bond between us.

"We've known each other a good while. You shouldn't feel awkward asking me a question. Please go ahead. I'll answer it as best I can. I don't talk much, and it's been a while since I've talked to another person except you. So I might not be able to express myself well, but I'll do my best."

Despite your willingness to answer my questions, I was still afraid to hurt your feelings. But in the end, my curiosity won out.

"How do you take care of yourself now?"

"I live with my mother. I'd say my mother was somewhat luckier than yours. She managed to get a divorce from my stepfather and used all her savings to buy this relatively inexpensive apartment before I was discharged from the hospital. Like I said earlier, she has chronic health problems. So sometimes one of my cousins comes and helps us out. I don't think you've seen my mom yet. She has to stay in bed most of the time. I stay with her during the day, talking and helping her as much as I can. Since I can't use my legs, I can only help with easy jobs such as combing her hair, clipping her nails, changing her clothes."

I wanted to ask you how you managed to support yourself economically, but I wasn't sure you'd want to answer such a personal question. Even if you did, I wouldn't be able to help you with anything.

While I was contemplating my next question, three metallic bangs rang out, indicating that it was 3 a.m. I knew we should end our conversation for the night, but neither of us seemed interested in sleep.

Your eyes were still shining in the dark. How could we abandon such a night?

My mind wasn't tired, but I realized that my body was longing for the warm morning hours. It was getting cold. I rubbed my fingers and toes to keep them warm. My legs started aching because I'd been sitting in the same position for so long. I briefly thought your legs must be aching too, then remembered that your legs weren't capable of feeling anything.

I silently cursed your stepfather and the man who attacked you for paralyzing your legs as well as your future. Your fingers should have been playing a guitar, and your feet should have been tapping out the rhythms of your songs as thousands of fans cheered for you on the stage. It was unbelievable how cruelly your destiny had been changed.

"Chu, you can still play the guitar, can't you?" My loud voice broke the silence.

Your reply was subdued. "You might think that my hands are completely fine, but they aren't. And even if they were, I don't ever want to hold a guitar again."

I'd messed up again. How could I forget that your guitar played a role in your tragedy? I found it difficult to continue the conversation, and the dawn brought us to silence again.

"Hey," you said, "I've been thinking. Maybe your stepfather and my stepfather are actually the same man?" I flinched, as you laughed it off with your usual non-poetic laughter.

Chu, that night's conversation made me think about you and your life more than ever.

## 6

The winter was retreating, the cold weather receding. I had nothing special to do in my room. My mind was busy, however, thinking about my future. I couldn't know for sure what it would bring, but I felt like I should prepare myself for every possible scenario and try my best to detach from the difficult situation I had been brought into. I had to gain confidence in my abilities. I knew that the current situation would not last forever.

As I thought of myself and my future, Chu, I couldn't help thinking of you and yours. You occupied a large part of my mind. To be honest, I preferred thinking about you and your future: I had a better chance of standing up for myself, on my own feet. But you, Chu...

People say that there's always hope and that one mustn't underestimate karma and destiny. You might meet a doctor someday who could treat your legs and make you healthy and happy again.

All human beings should hope for a better life. If I could, couldn't you? I wanted to know how you felt. I wanted you to have hope for your future, Chu.

My mind got so congested thinking about you, I had to find a way out. So I came out to the veranda looking for you, wanting to know how you felt about your future.

The sun was shining. It was as if the winter had never been. The whole world was sprinkled with sunshine under the blue sky. Green buds were sprouting on the trees and shrubs, and the slopes in the distance were ablaze with magnolia blossoms. Everything looked beautiful.

Being night owls, we had forgotten the beauty of the daytime. This one was magnificent.

You were not by the window. I thought about calling your name but didn't want to scare you. So I came up with a plan and went back into my room to fetch my guitar.

I started singing Sai Hti Saing's "Summer Morning," but the music meant to entice you caught me up in it's swirl instead. I was pulled into the song's melody and found myself singing wholeheartedly:

*"Like an ancient pristine day, the beauty of this summer morning is unparalleled,*
*But I happened to lie sleepless last night"*

At the end of the first verse, your face popped up near the window all lit up with delight. No wonder—after all, you were a music lover, so it's natural the music would draw you out.

*"Travelers with different destinations,*
*We meet here for only a short while,*
*My rendezvous with the summer morning didn't last for long"*

You sang the last verse of the song in a whisper. It made me happy, but singing that song was not my only mission that day.

I laid the guitar on the floor and stood up, holding the veranda rail with both hands. "Chu?"

"Yes?"

"If..." I paused for a moment. Contemplating if it was appropriate to ask you.

"Yes, I'm listening. If... what?"

I smiled vaguely, then finished my question. "If your legs were to become normal again, what would you do?"

You laughed, a sad broken laugh. "Do you think my legs will ever recover?"

I had expected such a response and tried harder to raise your hope.

"Who can predict the future? No one can say for sure that your legs will never recover. Maybe it's just not the right time and place yet. Maybe there are some competent doctors and technology out there that you don't know of yet. Maybe your condition can be cured. Please don't lose hope, Chu."

You seemed deep in thought. I hoped you were searching for a reason to keep hoping. I wanted to believe that my words could cheer you up.

"Did you hear me, Chu?"

"Yes, I heard you."

'We should think about the future, just in case. What do you want to do if your legs get better? What do you wish to do the most?"

"I want to sing."

"Good. What's next?"

"Then, I want to travel to Inlay Lake."

I was so happy your spirit was still intact enough to say such words. I kept going, wanting to do more.

"Okay, the first thing we'll do is travel to Inlay Lake. The nature's so beautiful there, it'll clear our minds, and we'll be able to imagine a new life and have the strength to do whatever we want.

"You'll play guitar for me when I sing, right?"

"Of course. I know there are other guitarists far better than me, but if you want me to play for you, I'll happily do it."

Your voice grew firmer and your eyes shone brighter, confusing me and making me wonder if I should feel happy or sad.

"Hey, you must come with me on tour around the country when I start getting requests."

I laughed to cover up my uncertainty. "Sure, I'll follow you wherever you go. But I'm afraid you'll no longer care for me once you become a very successful singer."

You started laughing. You were surfing wholeheartedly towards the future now, embracing all your dreams.

Surfing along with you on the waves of future, I became euphoric. Your soul-stirring voice coursing through the air. The electric guitars driving the beat. I imagined the thunderous applause of your fans, your non-poetic but enchanting laughter, my smile and our ecstasy.

I could hear my heart pounding with excitement. Even though the future is unpredictable, I couldn't stop expecting all this. How joyful it would be if we could realize our dreams. The sound of your laughter reverberating across Inlay Lake and your voice echoing among the temples of Bagan.

"I've never flown before. Let's fly together when we travel."

My happy thoughts landed at your feet, worshipping your confident words. Looking into your dancing eyes, I said, "Good. I have a friend at an airline office."

You laughed excessively, so much so I felt embarrassed.

"I'm not exaggerating, Chu. I'm just telling the truth."

You were laughing even more hysterically now.

"Uh, stop it, Chu."

Uncomfortable, I picked up my guitar. Disappointed at having my reverie broken and feeling slightly ashamed,

I resumed my guitar-playing and let my fingers pick out some tunes.

————————

"When you go back home, don't ever come back here." Your eyes were inscrutable as you spat out these words.

"Why do you say this?"

"Words like loneliness and solitude might sound beautiful in novels, but they taste bitter in reality," you said sadly, but with conviction.

At that moment you didn't look like a girl who was capable of singing exuberantly or laughing vibrantly. When you stopped pretending to be resilient, you suddenly became a melancholy young woman. How could I blame you?

What you said next surprised me.

"You told me we had to fight against injustice, that we both ended up here because we fought back. So now we must endure the suffering that those actions for justice have brought."

I was wondering how to respond to such adamant words, when you continued.

"I'm able to withstand the harshness of my life. That's how I continue to survive. I've been living with this condition for four years now. Sometimes it upsets me, wondering what people must think of me and what I did. Was I wrong to hurt him like that?" The rhetorical question shook your voice. Then you asked in a whisper, "What do you think of me?" My heart felt a sharp stabbing pain.

"Look, Chu. The one who would say you were wrong is someone who has never done a right thing."

You seemed to accept my unequivocal opinion. Having decided not to argue, you exhaled cigarette smoke and nodded.

"Hearing you say that makes me feel better, but I don't get a chance to hear other people's thoughts so much." Again, the pain stabbed my chest. I wanted to help you, but what could I do for you? How could I save you when I couldn't even save myself from the dark shadow over my own life?

"Please don't lose heart, Chu. Even if I go back home, I'll come back here often to see you. We can talk and sing, just like this now. I'll play music, and you can sing."

You burst into laughter again, recognizing that I was trying too hard to cheer you up. What you said next silenced me.

"I've adapted well to this place. I don't want to see you back here unless it's because you've made a conscious decision to fight injustice."

# 7

Do you believe people can have premonitions about the future? I've never experienced that much before, but this time I felt it quite distinctly.

When I heard the footsteps coming toward my room, I knew I'd be leaving that very day. I felt torn: happy about maybe returning to my family, but at the same time very sad to leave you, Chu.

The oily face of my stepfather appearing at the door chased away any momentary pride I had about my premonition being right. All I wanted was to call you so that I could point to him and say, "This is him—my stepfather."

But I didn't want to rouse you at this hour—night person that you were, so used to singing through the night and ignoring the daytime. I worried that waking you during the day would upset you and leave you depressed. Besides, we were both suffering from stepfather-hatred, so seeing his face would probably not do you any favors.

"Pack your stuff. You have to go home."

At first his command roused my will to resist. But my desire to see my mother and sister shot down this rebellious streak: I knew they'd be waiting for me eagerly, their only son and brother. Indeed, I was no longer sure I could ever stand up for my family against my stepfather again if the price to pay was this kind of solitary confinement.

Chu, I was genuinely sorry to leave you for my family and my future. My decision to leave you hurt me deeply.

I wanted very badly to see you one last time, to wave and smile at you sadly, to call out good-bye in a downhearted voice. Even if it were only a wild daydream, I wanted to tell you that your legs would be healthy again someday and that your father would soon find his way back home.

I wanted to see you face-to-face, to look into those eyes that could change colors so quickly, to see your purpled, cigarette-battered lips and your pale cheek with its dark little mole. I would have settled for a brief glance of your graceful eyes.

"What? You don't want to go home? Why are you so slow packing your things? You must want to stay here."

I tried to ignore him, still wrapped up in my thoughts about you. I didn't owe him any explanation about the contents of my heart, which knew well enough why I was dragging my feet, despite my excitement to reunite with my family.

My hands packed my things while my thoughts daydreamed about seeing you. If you came to the window right now, I'd point to him and say, "This is the guy who sent me here."

Would you thank him for letting me come into your life, even for a short moment? Or would you hate him for making my life miserable? I wish I had a chance to talk with you about it.

But it was too late for all that. After all, we were just two tiny human beings whose minds had to shuttle between happiness and sadness.

"Let's go."

Heavy-hearted, I rose slowly, looked at your window for a while and then headed toward the door.

"So long, Chu."

I realized that I was leaving behind all the things I adored: your voice, your songs, your non-poetic laughter. The slam of the door, no longer unfamiliar to me, and the click of the lock—those too would forever remain deep inside my heart.

---

I thought about you that night—how you would look at my room and expect me to come out.

The summer breeze would pass between our two buildings. The twinkling stars that had accompanied our nights would greet you as usual. The sky that had wrapped its arms around us would look for us again.

By now, you'd be waiting for my guitar, or maybe leaning against the backrest of your wheelchair lining up your words for the night. Or maybe you'd be keeping yourself busy figuring out what songs to sing tonight. When you were ready and I was still nowhere to be seen, you might start singing to let me know you were there.

Maybe you'd start with "Separated by Salween" or "Yearning for Home."

And when you'd exhausted all your favorite songs and I hadn't come out, what would you do? Would you gaze at my unlit room and grow worried that something bad had happened to me?

And when your staying power was worn out by the break of dawn, would you understand that the room was empty and I was gone?

Would you loathe me for leaving you without saying good-bye? Or would you burst into tears for having lost your only friend? Or would you mock your cruel fate with your non-poetic, sarcastic laughter?

I didn't think there would be any crying or laughing. You'd just sit by the window, your purple lips drawn tight.

I couldn't sleep that night, nor any other night for that matter. I stayed up thinking about the sleepless nights we spent together. No matter how sad it makes me to think about it, I always try to remember your words.

"Don't come back here again unless it is because you've made a conscious decision to fight injustice."

Your words gave me strength, Chu. I will always be indebted to you for these words.

## 8

It's totally dark tonight. Not even a hint of moonlight or a glimpse of stars. Thick dark clouds brimmed with rain hang over the city, which is eerily quiet.

I keep myself busy with such paltry little things these days, trying to forget you. I don't have the guts to cut you loose from my mind. How could I? I don't even have the guts to cut the strings that tether my own freedom. The fact that I have to try so hard to forget you is proof that I'm still not over you.

I wanted to come to see you, Chu. Truly. I miss them so much, our nights full of talking and singing, the kindness and gazes and smiles we shared.

But I know that you don't want to hear my excuses, so full of my own unsatisfied revenge. And I don't want to tell you about my life, which is again full of bitterness. Our lives were already full of those things; we don't need any more sorrow to drown in.

Our meeting should be redolent of happiness and pleasure. But I know any meeting between us would still be meaningful, even if we had nothing happy to say.

Tonight I walked by the neighborhood where you lived. My heart beat out of control when I turned into your street and saw the building you lived in with its many apartments, some lit up with lights and some not. All I could think about was whether your room was lit or not.

My insides were churning as I approached the small alley that separated our two buildings. It was quiet and mostly deserted.

There were no lights on in your room. The room I had lived in was also dark.

As it was already late, a calm prevailed over the neighborhood. This was the hour our conversations used to start.

From in front of the building I had lived in, I looked up at your window. My perspective from the alley didn't give me a sense of whether you could see the outside world from your window or not.

Staring at your window from a distance almost quenched my longing for you.

And you, Chu? How is it for you tonight? How you are defining your life? Are you busy planning your future, fickle though it may be? Or are you still struggling with your tragic past?

You told me once that you still expected your father to come back. Are you still counting on that return, Chu? Is that still the foundation of your dreams?

I don't know how to apologize for not keeping my promise to come back to this place regularly. Would you accept my failure with a sarcastic smile?

I've earned a degree but had to take a job that has nothing to do with my education. Unlike before, I now have a way of earning money, but it's hard to support myself, let alone my family. I still can't take full responsibility for my mother and sister, so I continue to watch them live in fear under the control of the man they despise.

Still burdened with the same problems, how dare I come back and show my face? How could a person like me with so many problems make you happy? What would happen when you see a man who can do nothing for you?

The pain of leaving someone again could cancel out all the happiness of a brief reunion. So I stayed away, Chu. I don't want to make your pain worse.

You might have forgotten about me. If so, then I want you to keep forgetting me. I never stop dreaming of the day I'll be capable of making you happier and your life better. When that day comes, I'll come back for you. This is the promise I've made to myself. We have to wait for that one day though.

As I stood there, the night became older. My neck was getting stiff from gazing up toward your window, but I couldn't get myself to stop staring. I wanted to see and feel your presence.

There was no way for you to know that the person who once cared for you was yet again so near. I couldn't expect to see any clear sign that you were there in the room. I don't remember how many times I sighed.

It began to drizzle; the cold sprinkles of rain felt soft on my face. It was a different coldness from the coldness I felt with you those winter nights.

The sky grew darker with the sound of thunder. The raindrops got bigger. I heard the metal strikes, letting me know it was two o'clock in the morning. This used to be the time we'd go to bed.

"Goodnight, Chu."

I wished you a happy and peaceful sleep. It was the second time I'd say goodbye without your knowing.

Don't miss me. Please try to forget me—I was only a small tiny patch on the canvas of your life.

I prepared to leave. For the last time ever, I gazed up at your window, and then I noticed . . .

"Oh…" My heart pounded harder, my legs felt stunned. All my senses snapped to full attention.

Yes. It was cigarette smoke drifting out of your window! I could see it distinctly even in the rain and darkness. You were still awake! I pictured you with the cigarette between your purple lips.

With a flash of thunder, the sky suddenly poured down—a rain so strong it obliterated my view of the smoke. I couldn't blame the rain. How could it know  I had spent so many hours waiting to see such a sign?

How unfortunate we have been, Chu.

We have been unfortunate enough not even to know whom to blame for our suffering.

It was exhilarating to turn my face toward the sky and feel the touch of the raindrops that must have passed through your cigarette smoke.

The raindrops were cold, but when I closed my eyes, I felt a mysterious kind of warmth run down over my eyelids and cheeks.

*Khet Mar*

# Life on Death Row

*Where mental torture is the punishment for minor infringements of prison regulations*

* This piece was originally published in *Irrawaddy Magazine*.

The cell I was allotted measured about 15 square feet with a row of metal bars forming one wall. It was lit by a 40-watt bulb. One corner had a bamboo mat where my cellmate, a young woman, sat. I joined her, sitting on one corner of the mat and answered her questions: "Who are you? What interrogation center did you come from? How was your interrogation?" We chatted, describing our experiences. I described the beatings and kicks, and she showed me how her fingers had been injured by her interrogators with a sharp piece of bamboo.

Around 8 p.m., as the prison fell into silence, I heard knocks on the back wall of the cell. My companion knocked back in reply—this was apparently one method the prisoners used to communicate. We were also able to talk directly through the bars to three young women in a cell facing ours. We talked into the night and finally turned in around 2 a.m. I found it difficult to sleep in these new surroundings with the light burning all night.

The prison was awake early, and there was activity outside our cell. A plate of warm porridge was served up at 7 a.m. Around 10 a.m., I heard rhythmic shouts of what sounded like "Take!" and "Pour!" accompanied by the splashing of water from a yard beyond our cell. Curious to know what the commotion meant, I unfastened a window at the top of one of the cell walls and peered out. About 20 women were splashing themselves with water from a brick tank, supervised by a cane-wielding prison guard who was shouting the commands, "Take!" and "Pour!" At the command "Take!" the women would scoop water from the tank; they then splashed themselves clean with it when the warden yelled "Pour!"

As I watched that strange scene, I heard a loud voice behind me. "Who opened the window?" It was a guard.

I had unfastened the window by untying a piece of metal wire that secured its two handles and then sliding back the bolt. "I opened it," I confessed.

"Who ordered you to do that?" the guard barked.

"It was just a window," I protested. Where was the harm in opening it? But opening a window was apparently a cardinal crime, earning me a haranguing from the guard who then condemned me to be transferred to the prison's "Death Row."

I picked up my small pile of clothes, bid goodbye to my cellmate and the three inmates of the neighboring cell and followed a guard to my new, ominously named quarters.

Death Row was a brick building divided by a narrow passageway and lined by five small cells and two larger ones. As its chilling name implied, it housed prisoners sentenced to death. And now I was one of them.

I was assigned to one of the larger cells, which measured about 20 feet by 12 feet. About ten women shared the cell. They gave me a noisy welcome, showering me with questions. Within one week, all but two of them had been led away.

The cell, in which I was to spend several months, had a slop pail in one corner and a pot of drinking water in another. We shared three plates and two bamboo mats, surviving on a diet of boiled peas, spinach, sour soup, fried prawn paste and tamarind. When we were let out of the cells to cross the yard to the shower, we collected what vegetables and greens we could find to add some variety to our meals, using a knife fashioned from a hair clip to cut the meager produce.

Sometimes women who received food parcels from visiting family members shared such treats as homemade curry, fish paste and fried vegetables. I noticed, however, that the parcels weren't as big or as appetizing when they were brought in by the husbands of the imprisoned women.

One woman inmate told me, "When men are imprisoned, their wives struggle to visit them, despite many difficulties. But when women are imprisoned, their husbands only try to be dutiful. They make excuses about caring for the children, household work and daily chores. Some husbands even take up with another woman."

We had some freedom on Death Row—freedom to talk and argue among ourselves. And to pray. I still didn't know how long I would have to serve in prison. And why Death Row? It was not a good omen.

There were worse places to be, however. One punishment cell was a dark, windowless place with a floor of wet sand. Four or five days in this dank, fetid hole were the punishment for violating prison regulations.

At night, we boosted our spirits by singing. Some of the inmates knew the popular songs of performers like Zaw Win Hut and Hay Mar Ne Win, and they had good voices too.

I'm no singer, so I related some of the books I had read.

After four months, just as I was getting used to the routine on Death Row, my name was called, and I was escorted to a jeep parked at the prison entrance. The jeep took me to another prison building where two intelligence officers, two soldiers and a woman guard accompanied me inside. It was crowded with students, all waiting to appear before a prison court martial.

I can't remember the details of the charges against me—only the sentence. Ten years. At least now the uncertainty was over. As the sun set on a hot summer day, I was led away to begin my prison term, not on Death Row but in a special ward for women prisoners.

# Night Flow

* This piece was originally published in *Warscape Magazine*.

I sat on the bank of the slow-swirling river, shoulders hunched and fists and teeth clenched against the bone-chilling night breeze. The stone bench was as cold as a block of ice, or so I thought. The cold breeze blowing across the river touched my bare neck, giving me goose bumps.

A river is always bigger than a creek or stream, I was taught. The Iowa River reminded me of Maletto, the stream that flows behind the long-stilted house where I lived until my teens. My village is also called Maletto. Maletto's water is not clear: it is muddied in the rainy season and almost-clear in the summer. On both its banks, an unending patchwork of rice-paddies, sunflowers, chilies and peanuts abound. My village friends who couldn't afford school tended these fields all year round, but my sister and I were lucky because our mother was a teacher at the village school. During the summer holidays, we joined my friends in picking chilies. The sun baked our supple bodies and the hot chillies in our tender hands. When we had filled a sack, we were paid a small basketful of chilies in return. We could keep our share to use ourselves, sell it at the market nearby, or sell it back to the owner. Most of us kept what we needed and sold the rest back to the farmer.

At noon we would break for lunch—rice, fish paste, vegetables and miniscule portions of fish caught from the Maletto creek—brought to us, sometimes in aluminum containers but mostly in the traditional wrapping of inn leaves, by our group of friends. We sat under the shade of a huge tree sharing our food, laughing and teasing each other. It was the best part of the day. After lunch, we returned to the fields leaving the soiled inn leaves on the ground.

In 2001, after being gone for five years, I revisited my stilt village and discovered that plastic bags had replaced the inn leaves. The hot air blew the bags over the fields where we had once laughed together.

"Why?" I asked my friend Ma Khin Maw.

She looked at me strangely. "Where else would we throw them?"

I stared at her, thinking she was the strange one with her nonchalant acceptance that plastic could replace the leaves. The people of my village are just as apathetic about the mangrove that grows along Maletto's swamps. The villagers themselves chopped the mangroves down to make charcoal, whose sale lined the pockets of businessmen. Now its marine life is slowly disappearing and the villagers find fewer fish and shrimp to eat, a staple they used to enjoy. Mangrove swamps also act as barriers to protect the villages against storms or tsunami that come in from the Indian Ocean.

Don't my people realize what they are doing?

Working for a handful of rice in order to survive becomes an isolated act in the darkness.

The day after I arrived at Iowa University, I went on a field trip with the other participants of the International Writing Program to the Red Bird Farm.

Yes! I was walking on American soil in the American wilds. I was in the fields of Maletto without plastic bags.

As we strolled along, a fellow writer walking in front of me threw an empty plastic water bottle into the thick grass.

Seconds later: "Who threw this?"

"I'm sorry," was the honorable admission.

"Please don't do that," the dark-haired young woman with a nose-ring said sternly. She looked young enough to be in her late teens. She picked up the bottle as if she were lifting an ugly thing from a bed of exotic flowers.

———————

As teenagers, whenever we had free time, my friends and I fished in the Maletto creek. I used a light pole, but they would go right in, searching for fish with their hands and feet, snatching the fish up on contact. They could name them without even looking, yelling, "It's a catfish!" or "A *ngazinyaing*!" Usually they were right. I had no such skill. They would throw the mud-coated fish to me on the bank, and I would put it in a bamboo basket. My grandmother scolded me for aiding in a taking of life, something we Buddhists were not supposed to do. But picking up the fish was so exciting, I didn't pay any attention to her.

I imagined how exciting it would be to grab the fish in the water as the others did. Then one day May Tin Aye threw a *ngazinyaing*, a dwarf catfish, up to me, and its dorsal fin caught my big toe. The toe swelled up, and I cried all night because it burned and hurt so bad.

My grandmother crushed some medicinal herbs to fight the poison.

"This is retribution, you know," she said. "You have pain in your little toe; think of the fish suffering in the basket."

Still crying from the pain and the scolding, I listened to her. But since I was not a fish, I could not fathom the suffering of fish. I thought instead how the fish that my friends caught would be sold and turned into money. The cash would buy rice, and with the hollow-stemmed vegetables that grew abundantly in their backyards, they would make a meal to support their lives. I confess my lack of feeling for fish. I was sad and angry that my friends couldn't even afford to eat what they caught. Many of my friends are still in this sad situation, along with many others whom I don't know as well. My thoughts returned to my toe. Strangely, the heat and pain had died away. My foot was cooler again, and I felt better.

One night on the bank of the Iowa River, the tip of my toe felt another warm sensation. By the light of the lamppost about twenty feet away, I looked down and could see a rabbit examining my foot with its nose. Dark grey with quick eyes and upright ears, the rabbit looked back at me. How tame it was. I sat without moving. But my toe was no kind of food, so he hopped into the misty grasses nearby.

That very evening I had also seen furry-tailed squirrels running and playing along the bank, as well as ducks on the river. Some fought for food, some for love, and some were just playing. Was this really America? It felt like the jungle grove where I cut *taryor* branches to prepare local shampoo for my grandmother.

But I am in America, actual America, I thought, readjusting my thoughts.

That night, around midnight, I connected with my friend in Burma through Google Talk.

"How is Iowa"?

"Very nice! Lots of ducks in the river, also squirrels, and rabbits, too."

"Really! I wish we had that in Burma!"

I imagined he envied the peaceful scene, but wasn't quite sure, so I asked "Why?"

"Well, you can cook and eat them. Rabbit is delicious, and duck so tasty!"

I had nothing to say in return. **But I wondered, what had happened to those noted Burmese traits of kindness and blamelessness? Had they been defeated?**

**On the other hand, I reasoned, if people had enough to eat, he wouldn't have had such awful designs on my tranquil scene.** I giggled at his comment—and I wanted to cry.

I don't know why I want to cry so much in Iowa.

———————

Last night I cried. That was the night of September 26th.

Earlier I'd had two glasses of white wine at a gathering, which had warmed me to the sudden change of weather: As sun melts ice, the wine melted my sadness into tears. It had been good to hold many warm hands that night—hands from Argentina, the Czech Republic, Russia, Malta, Montenegro, Malaysia, Hong Kong, hands full of compassion from around the world. Their warmth and kindness reached deep inside me. They understood. They could feel what I felt. It was palpable.

This love is also like a gift to my Burmese people, which I will take back with me to Burma.

Those warm hands understand the story of my Burmese friend Kaythi, now living in Oslo, who called me in Iowa when she heard I was here. **Having been granted political asylum in Norway, she doesn't know when she will step on our own soil again. Perhaps one day when Burma attains democracy.** She told me about her life in Oslo, starting with the severe cold and her struggle to survive and be happy.

"I was at a small party," she told me, "like a family gathering. It was nice. The kids played about on the lawn. The grown-ups drank wine and talked. I was thinking that life is worth living after all, then suddenly I thought of Burma and my family and friends there. And here I was sipping wine and feeling happy. My mother has become a seller in the market. **My friend is hiding to avoid being arrested. She's left her little daughter behind. The baby cries constantly for her mother's milk, and the mother's breasts ache because her daughter isn't there to nurse. She doesn't know where she will sleep from one night to the next. And the rest of my friends in Burma are either imprisoned or at the interrogation centers. I can hardly bear it."**

Kaythi sobbed. Her sobs were like electricity slicing through the air to me. I was tormented after our phone call and had no one close to share my sorrow. I could see the tears on Kaythi's thick lashes and started to cry myself.

"My dear friend, what happened?" asked a friend from Montenegro.

"She needs to cry," said a Russian friend.

"We're with you. Okay?" another told me.

Oh! How good to have a family. Then the thought of my family and friends in Burma struck my heart, and a rush of loneliness overwhelmed the comfort I had just received. And yet, all of us from all over the world, are one family now. Destiny brought us here. Soon we will return to our homes, but I am very fortunate to have these friends who will gather up my tears and the tears of Burma with their warm hands.

I never cry in Burma. I don't know why I lack the strength to cry. Sometimes, lying next to my little boy, I feel like it, but just weep gently so as not to wake him. Though I would like to shoot my splintered thoughts across the galaxy, I lie still on my bamboo mat, inhaling my sighs.

In Iowa, I cry to my heart's content. I sob and wipe away the tears over and over until my tear ducts are dry. I run myself into the ground with crying and then, completely knocked out, I fall asleep peacefully like my little son.

One dawn I woke up in high spirits after a good sleep and decided to write. Suddenly I saw an old woman wearing dark clothes and sitting comfortably with one knee up on the end of my bed, her eyes fixed on me. A young woman in a red dress, perhaps a teenager, stood in front of the window leaning on the windowsill and smiling at me.

Who are these people, I wondered and rose swiftly to switch on the table lamp next to my bed. Through the curtainless window, yellow light from the lampposts shown into my room.

"Well, the old one in black isn't the black refrigerator opposite my bed. Certainly not. So who are they?" I wondered.

I had met the figure of this old woman once before—at a meditation center in Pathein. For the breathing exercise, there are two methods: sitting down or walking to and fro. I favored the latter, for which there is a pathway you can follow. One day as I was walking the path meditating, I saw an old woman dressed in a dark brown robe, what we call a Yogi-colored robe, leaning against a pole. But I didn't see her with my eyes; I saw her in my mind, in a kind of trance. I concentrated on every step: lifting my foot, moving forward, stepping down. Lift... move...and step...

Slowly, I approached her. When I was less than an arm's length away, she touched my shoulder with her hand. I looked up. It wasn't a woman but a skeleton that had touched me. I reasoned hard: My mind was making me see things. I pulled myself together and concentrated on my breathing.

Breathe in... breathe out.

Breathe in... breathe out.

I told a friend from Europe about the dawn encounter with the two women.

"Were your eyes closed or opened when you saw them?"

"I don't remember."

"Well, it was a dream."

Instantly, I recalled what a woman had told me fifteen years earlier—someone who had helped me in my life: "My sister, you are being taken care of by women from the unseen place. You will meet them often, either in your dreams or in your thoughts."

"Yes,' I told her. "I see these women in my dreams quite often, including my grandmother. They always seem to be watching me. Why is that?"

"Perhaps they want to protect you. Or they want something from you."

"Yes," I whispered back.

It seemed most likely that they wanted to protect me from the consequences of my own actions. I don't think they wanted anything from me. I recite holy verses every night to entreat that others may benefit equally from my prayer. I have only this deed to offer. It is good that these women are protecting me. But there are also many men who have helped me. I must be a lucky person.

And yet, I know there are people watching me who do not watch out of love.

---

Like magic with its enchantment of color, Iowa's early autumn gives way to winter. It's not easy for this Burmese girl who came from temperatures of 104 degrees Farenheit to live in 40-degree-Farenheit weather. My hands and feet chill quickly in my room. When I look outside, I love seeing the bright rays of the sunlight that I used to loathe in sizzling Burma. Sun eases the cold, but the breeze is chilling.

From my window, I watch the Iowa, a river I have come to love. It has become my companion.

I recall the words of my friend, the poet Ra Hee Duk, from South Korea, who said, "You must really be in love with the river, Khet."

"Yes, I am."

"The flowing water at night is fascinating. The surface is supple and calm. But underneath runs restless water struggling to find its freedom. Only those who love and observe the river can perceive this phenomenon." As she said this, she smiled, and the yellow light from the lampposts embraced the sliding night waters. I see her face, and her words reverberate in my mind.

When I get my fill of the river, I return to my room.

Here I read, write, think of my two sons, watch TV, listen to news; my mind wanders, I sigh, I cry, I use Google Talk.

**At bedtime, I nestle under my thick blanket and hear voices and see images—voices and images of despair from across our world. Who is causing this despair? "Them"? Or are we letting it happen? Dream and reality have become one.** In our world things happen when you don't want them to, and things don't happen when you want them to. But the promise of love chases the demons from my mind.

I lie still beneath the heavy blanket, although my sadness and worry are alert and kicking. I have become the night flow of the river beneath the surface, engaged in a skirmish with the current. I pray that those voices and images of distress drift away on the tranquil surface.

And I pray. I pray for their peace and mine. May all living things be at peace?

**Khet Mar** is a Burmese journalist, novelist, short story writer, poet, and essayist who has written about the true lives of ordinary people and the current situation in Burma. Trained as a chemist, Khet Mar embarked on a writing career and published the novel *Wild Snowy Night*, three collections of short stories and a volume of essays. Her works have been translated into Japanese, Spanish, and English, broadcasted and made into a short film in Japan. In 2007 she participated in the prestigious International Writing Program at the University of Iowa.

In addition to her writing, Khet Mar is a community developer and environmental activist. She is one of the founders of the Zagawa Environment Network, which brings together writers and journalists focusing on environmental issues in the region.

She was also a volunteer teacher for a school aimed to help young children living with HIV/AIDS and worked as an organizer for other Monastic Orphanage Education

Schools in Rangoon, Burma.  In 2009 she was a featured writer at the PEN Word Voices Festival.

From 2009 to 2012 she was a writer-in-residence at City of Asylum in Pittsburgh, which provides sanctuary to writers exiled under threat of severe persecution in their native countries. Khet Mar currently works for Radio Free Asia in Washington, D.C..

# Sampsonia Way Publishing

**Sampsonia Way** is the publishing arm of City of Asylum. It's a home for the work of exiled and endangered writers around the world; it publishes banned books in translation and anthologies of contemporary writing from countries where free speech is under threat, and it serves a global community of readers and writers through the online literary journal, SampsoniaWay.org.

# City of Asylum

**City of Asylum** provides long-term sanctuary to endangered literary writers, along with a broad range of residencies and programs in a community setting to encourage cross-cultural exchange. We also anchor neighborhood economic development by transforming blighted properties into homes for our literary-based programs, energizing public spaces through public art with text-based components.

City of Asylum is a 501(c)(3) nonprofit. To learn more about us and our programs, please visit our website: cityofasylumpittsburgh.org.

# A Special Thanks

In celebration of City of Asylum's 10th anniversary on October 18, 2014, our publishing arm, Sampsonia Way has published English translations of the writing that caused the persecution of the writers who came to live at our program in Pittsburgh. Thanks to...

## Exiled Voices Series Patrons
James Abraham
Scott Lamie

## Exiled Voices Series Sponsors
Owen Cantor
Joanne Leedom-Acketman
Bill Steen Jr.

## Patrons
Laurie Shearer

## Sponsors
Jonathan Arac
Adel Fougnies & Richard Thomas
Pam Goldman
Tienchi Martin-Liao
Christine Stingely

## Donors
Jane Bernstein
Valerie Bacharach
Marla Druzgal
Bridget Meeds
Barbara Talerico
Kelly Thomas
Nancy Reese

## The Conspiracy, a novel by Israel Centeno

"His fleshy, psychologically penetrating work is one of the great un-discovered literary experiences of Latin America."
   —Aurelio Major, Co-founding editor of *Granta en Español*

## Generation Zero: An Anthology of New Cuban Fiction
### Edited by Orlando Luis Pardo Lazo

"In Generation Zero, sarcasm, deterritorialization, transvestism, fragmentation, colloquialism, hybridization, adventure and imagination are redesigning Cuban identity, recovering their power of subversion and resignifying Utopia."
   —Paulo Antonio Paranaguá, *Le Monde*

Made in the
USA
Lexington, KY